See Them Grow

CHICKEN

by Joyce Markovics

Consultant: Phillip J. Clauer
Poultry Extension Specialist, Department of Animal Science
The Pennsylvania State University
University Park, Pennsylvania

BEARPORT PUBLISHING

New York, New York

Credits

Cover, © Menna/Shutterstock; Title Page, © S-F/Shutterstock; TOC, © pongwan sukpoka/Shutterstock; 4, © JIANG HONGYAN/Shutterstock; 4–5, © Tsekmister/Shutterstock; 6–7, © Rashid Valitov/Shutterstock; 8, © Eric Isselee/Shutterstock; 9, © Bananaboy/Shutterstock; 10, © therry/iStock; 11T, © Tsekhmister/Shutterstock and © Lubava/Shutterstock; 11B, © Jerome Wexler/Science Source, © smuayc/Dreamstime, and © Eivaisla/Shutterstock; 12T, © Lotus Images/Shutterstock; 12BL, © Jerome Wexler/Science Source and © Eivaisla/Shutterstock; 12BR, © E.R. Degginger/Science Source and © Eivaisla/Shutterstock; 13, © Jerome Wexler/Science Source and © Eivaisla/Shutterstock; 14–15, © saied shahin kiya/Shutterstock; 16, © saied shahin kiya/Shutterstock; 17, © saied shahin kiya/Shutterstock; 18, © yevgeniy11/Shutterstock; 19, © Epitavi/Shutterstock; 20, © DebbiSmirnoff/iStock; 21, © otsphoto/Shutterstock; 22 (background), © pongwan sukpoka/Shutterstock; 22 (T to B), © A_Lesik/Shutterstock, © cynoclub/Shutterstock, and © Shotgun/Shutterstock; 23 (T to B), © bananaboy/Shutterstock, © Aksenova Natalya/Shutterstock, © Jerome Wexler/Science Source, © HalynaBahlyk/Shutterstock, and © Vasin Lee/Shutterstock; 24, © Szasz-Fabian Jozsef/Shutterstock.

Publisher: Kenn Goin
Senior Editor: Joyce Tavolacci
Creative Director: Spencer Brinker
Design: Debrah Kaiser
Photo Researcher: Thomas Persano

Library of Congress Cataloging-in-Publication Data

Names: Markovics, Joyce L., author.
Title: Chicken / by Joyce Markovics.
Description: New York, New York : Bearport Publishing, 2017. | Series: See them grow | Includes bibliographical references and index. | Audience: Ages 5 to 8.
Identifiers: LCCN 2016038815 (print) | LCCN 2016045861 (ebook) | ISBN 9781684020423 (library) | ISBN 9781684020942 (ebook)
Subjects: LCSH: Chickens—Development—Juvenile literature.
Classification: LCC SF487.5 .M37 2017 (print) | LCC SF487.5 (ebook) | DDC 636.5—dc23
LC record available at https://lccn.loc.gov/2016038815

For more information, write to Bearport Publishing Company, Inc., 45 West 21st Street, Suite 3B, New York, New York 10010. Printed in the United States of America.

10 9 8 7 6 5 4 3 2 1

Contents

Chicken

A chicken looks for a juicy bug to eat.

The bird has a large body, small wings, and a **beak.**

How did it get that way?

Chickens, like robins and eagles, are a kind of bird.

A chicken starts its life as a tiny **embryo** inside an egg.

An embryo is formed when female and male chickens **mate.**

A female chicken is called a hen. A male chicken is called a rooster.

The egg develops in the female's body.

How?

A hen is born with thousands of tiny **yolks.**

Each day, her body releases one yolk inside her body.

Then, a clear liquid called **albumen** surrounds the yolk.

Finally, everything is covered with a hard shell.

It can take up to 32 hours for a hen's body to create an egg.

After the egg is fully formed, the hen squeezes it out of her body.

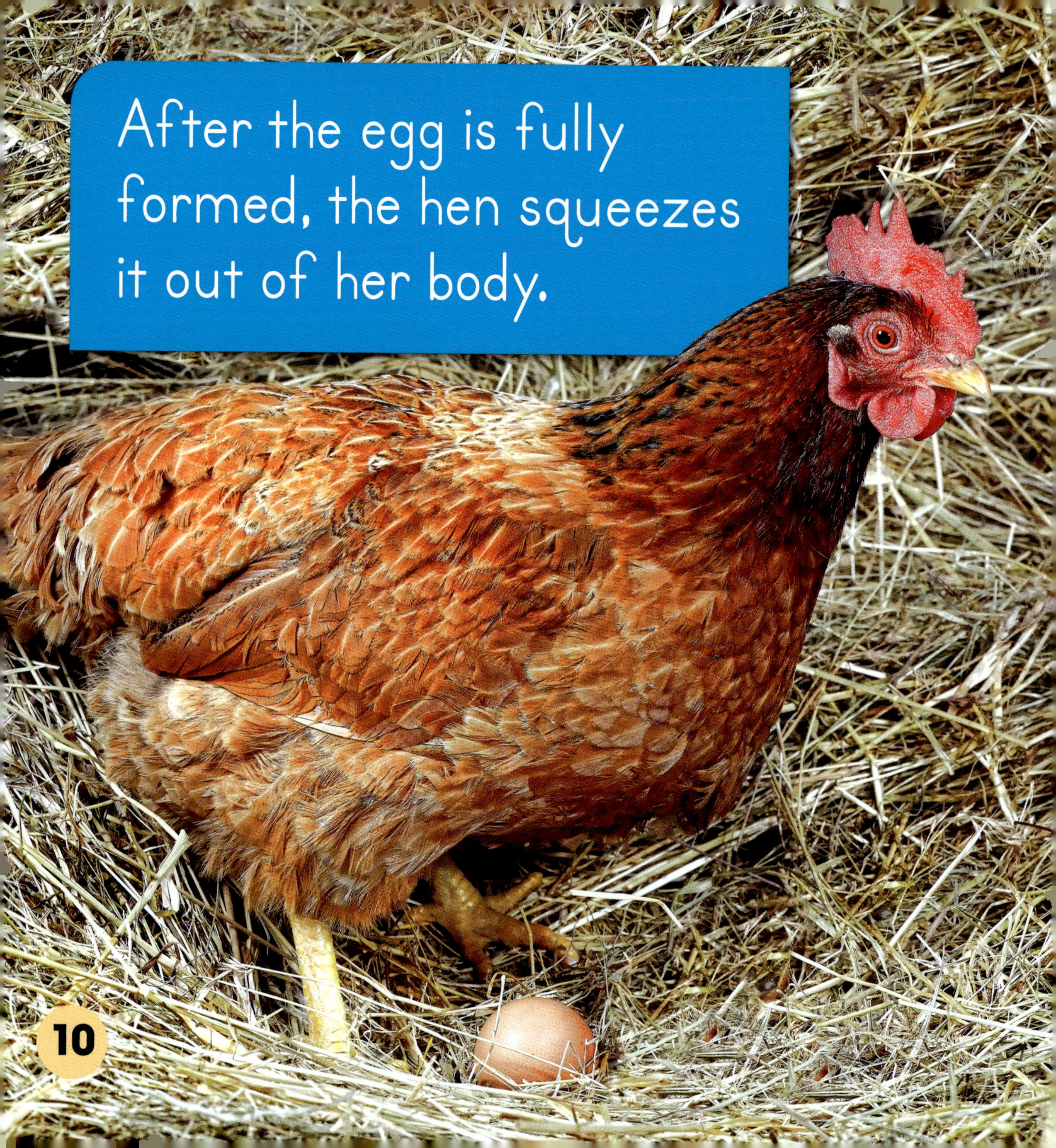

Then she sits on it to keep it warm.

Inside the egg, an embryo starts to grow.

embryo after 24 hours

An egg must be kept at about 99.5°F (37.5°C) for 21 days in order to hatch.

After a week, the embryo is the size of a lima bean.

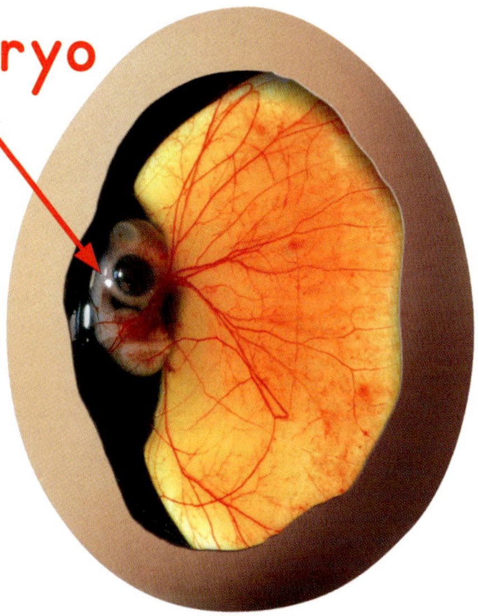

embryo: 6 days

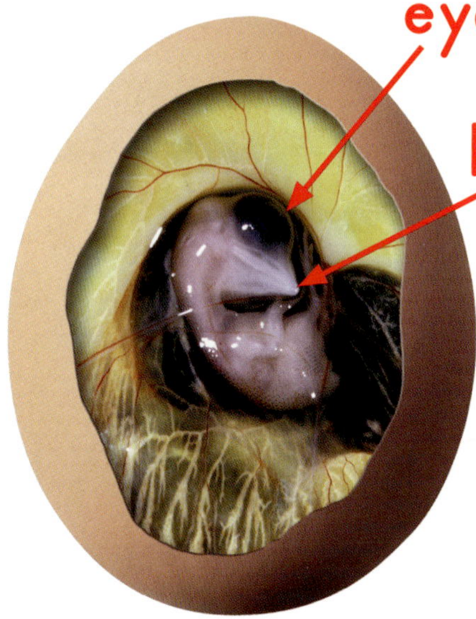

embryo: 9 days

The chick's eyes and beak begin to form.

The embryo grows bigger each day.

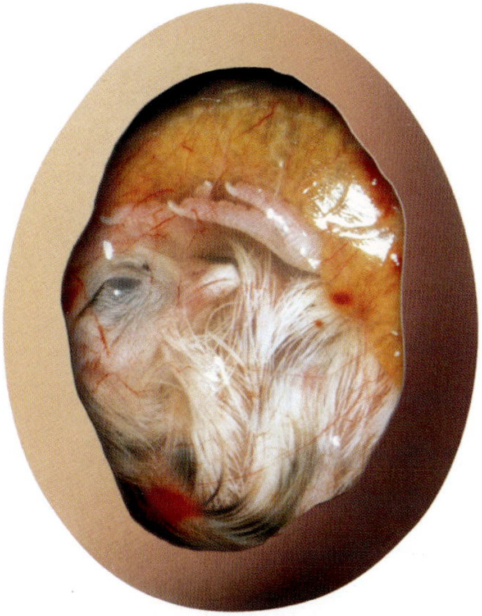

embryo: 17 days

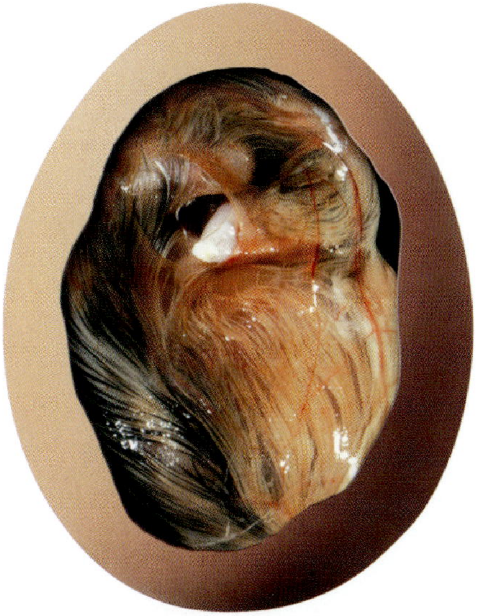

embryo: 20 days

By two weeks, it looks like a tiny bird.

On day 19, chicks can peep from inside their eggs!

On day 21, the chick is ready to hatch!

Peck, peck, peck.

It uses the tip of its beak to break the eggshell.

The tip of a chick's beak is called an egg tooth.

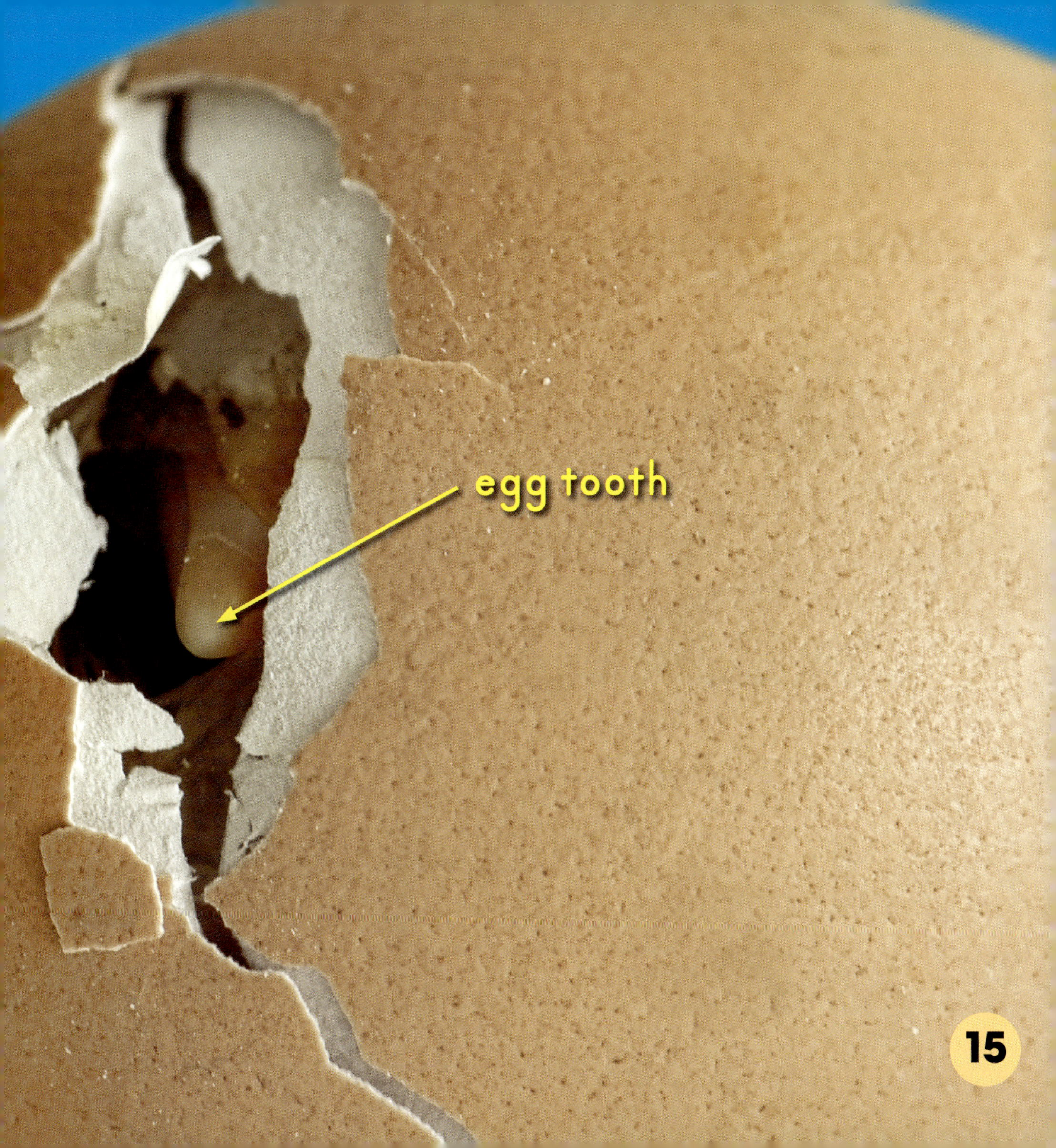
egg tooth

Finally, a large hole appears in the shell.

The chick breaks free!

Its body is covered with tiny feathers called down.

The chick's down is wet when it hatches.

Soon, the chick's feathers dry.

The baby bird starts moving around.

At first, its legs are wobbly.

Then the newborn gets more steady.

The chick looks for food.

A chick pecks the ground looking for food—just like an adult chicken.

After about six weeks, new feathers grow.

The young chicken's body gets larger.

In about six months, the chick will be fully grown!

Adult chickens have small wings. They can fly—just not very well!

Chicken Facts

- There are more than 350 different kinds of chickens.
- A hen can produce 150 to 300 eggs per year.
- A hen can lay an egg every day—even if she hasn't mated with a rooster!
- The heaviest chicken egg ever laid weighed nearly 1 pound (0.5 kg).

Glossary

albumen (al-BYOO-muhn) the clear liquid inside an egg

beak (BEEK) the hard, horn-shaped part of a bird's mouth

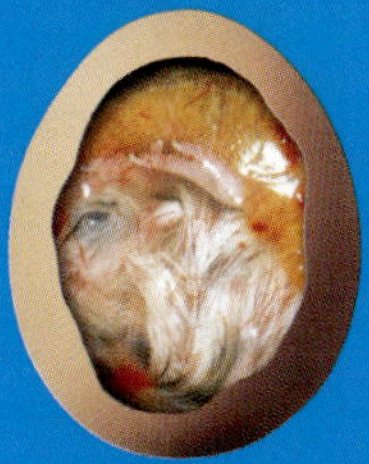

embryo (EM-bree-oh) an animal in the first stage of development

mate (MAYT) to come together to have young

yolks (YOHKS) the yellow parts of eggs that feed the growing embryos

Index

Read More

Ganeri, Anita. *From Egg to Chicken (How Living Things Grow).* Portsmouth, NH: Heinemann (2006).

Lundgren, Julie K. *Chickens (Life Cycles).* Vero Beach, FL: Rourke (2011).

Sklansky, Amy E. *Where Do Chicks Come From? (Let's-Read-and-Find-Out Science 1).* New York: HarperCollins (2005).

Learn More Online

To learn more about chickens, visit
www.bearportpublishing.com/SeeThemGrow

About the Author

Joyce Markovics lives in a very old house in Ossining, New York. One day, she hopes to raise fancy chickens called silkies and Polish frizzles.